ESKIMO SURPRISE

Patrick Skene Catling

Illustrated by
MARK FOREMAN

First published in Great Britain 1993
by William Heinemann Ltd
an imprint of Reed Consumer Books Ltd
Michelin House, 81 Fulham Road, London SW3 6RB

AUCKLAND   MELBOURNE   SINGAPORE   TORONTO

ISBN 0 434 96265 1

Printed in Italy
by Olivotto

A school pack of Banana Books 55–60
is available from
Heinemann Educational Books
ISBN 0 435 00109 4

Chapter 1

WHEN MIKE VERITY went with his
mother to the supermarket one Saturday
morning he found something really
fantastic.

His mother and father were going out
to dinner that evening and Mum had told
him: 'We're leaving you at home with
Gran tonight, so would you like to choose
something special for your supper?'

Wandering on his own along the aisles, he came to a freezer he had never noticed before. It was in a corner right at the back of the shop. In the freezer there was an exciting looking orange and pink packet labelled: ESKIMO SURPRISE – *A Rare Delicacy from the Frozen North.*

Mike grabbed it from the cold, caught up with his mother and tossed the frosty packet onto the heap of groceries in her trolley.

Early that evening, Mike's mother and father were ready to leave. 'You can ask Gran if you need anything,' his mother said. 'She's up in her room, reading. Your supper's on the kitchen counter.'

As soon as the car had gone, Mike ran to get the ESKIMO SURPRISE.

He was just lifting a plate from the shelf when he heard a faint tapping from inside the box. And then, to his amazement, he heard a small, anxious voice.

'Help!' it said. 'Get me out of here!'

Slowly Mike put his thumb under the flap and opened the packet. He had expected the surprise to be some unusual food. He certainly wasn't ready for anything as surprising as this.

A creature the size of a sparrow squeezed through the open end and jumped lightly on to the table. The creature had a pointed yellow beak and small, shiny eyes like a bird's, dark-grey leathery wings like a bat's, a smooth green body and tail like a lizard's, and a bird's thin legs and feet. It vigorously shook itself, scattering drops of water.

'Phew!' it exclaimed, obviously relieved. 'Thanks a lot! It was getting too cramped for comfort in there.'

A talking bird! Mike could hardly believe his good luck. He had heard that some parrots can be taught to say a few words. But here was something much better.

'What sort of bird are you?' he asked. 'Where are you from? I've never seen anything like you.'

'There are probably plenty of things you've never seen before. I'm a pterodactyl.' The word was pronounced *terro-dack-till.* 'We invented flying. I was born millions of years ago, at the time of

the dinosaurs. You know about them,
don't you?'

'Yes,' Mike said. 'We're learning about
dinosaurs at school.'

'Well, I fell through the ice and got stuck, frozen and preserved, in the Arctic, not far from the North Pole – until recently. Sometimes there are earthquakes deep down that stir things up. Fishermen, now and then, catch strange things in their nets. An Eskimo got me and sent me to your country.'

'How can you talk?' Mike wondered.

'When you live a few million years, you're sure to learn a thing or two,' the pterodactyl said modestly, without explaining exactly how.

'Are you a boy or girl?' Mike asked. The pterodactyl smiled.

'I'm a female,' she said. 'My mother used to call me Tilly. You can, if you like. What's your name?'
Mike told her.

'Is there anything to eat, Mike? It's been a long time since my last meal.'

'Of course, Tilly. What would you like? There's some chocolate ice-cream.'

'I used to eat dinosaur mostly. After their fights, there was always a lot of dinosaur lying about. But I'm so hungry I'll eat anything that's handy.'

Mike made her a strawberry jam sandwich, which she gobbled down.

'Thanks,' she said. 'Now I don't suppose you have anything meaty?'

Mike looked in the fridge and found some ham. He cut a piece into small squares and put them on a plate.

'Excuse me,' he said. 'I won't be long.' Leaving Tilly happily pecking away, he went upstairs to his grandmother's sitting-room.

'Gran!' he shouted as he burst open her door. 'I've got a pterodactyl! She's millions of years old!'

Mike's grandmother was a splendid, absent-minded lady. She was sitting in an armchair by a window reading poetry and listening to a tape of music. Her cat, Oliver, was resting at her feet.

The cat looked up at Mike, but his grandmother did not.

'That's nice,' she murmured, continuing to read her book.

'A pterodactyl, Gran! Honestly! Her name's Tilly. She talks! Don't you want to come and see her?'

His grandmother raised her head, peered over her glasses and kindly smiled at him. Oliver stood up, stretched, yawned, and casually strolled from the room.

'Yes, of course, dear,' she said.

'Gran! There's a real, live pterodactyl in the kitchen! I made her a jam sandwich.'

His grandmother frowned.

'Oh dear,' she said, 'I've forgotten to feed Oliver again. Please give him a piece of chicken from the fridge, and a saucer of milk.'

Oliver! Mike suddenly realised where the cat must have gone. 'Oh, no!' he exclaimed, and he turned and ran downstairs.

He hurried into the kitchen just as

Oliver leaped from the sink to the top of the highest cupboard. Tilly was already up there, with her back to the corner. Oliver prowled slowly towards her. He was preparing to pounce when . . .

'Oliver!' Mike yelled. 'Stop that at once! Get down!'

The cat knew perfectly well that he was not supposed to get on to the sink, let alone the cupboard. He reluctantly turned and jumped down.

'Out of the kitchen!' Mike ordered. The cat left, the door was shut, and Tilly flew down to the table.

'I'm sorry,' Mike said. 'Oliver's a good cat, but I should have thought.'

'That was an awkward moment,' Tilly said. 'He's a very good jumper. Anyway, no hard feelings. You can't blame a cat for being a cat.'

'I wonder if there's somewhere outside where I could live?' Tilly asked, 'Nothing fancy, you know, but cooler. And secure.'

Mike thought for a while, then clapped his hands together and grinned.

'I've got the perfect place. Come with me.'

He held out a hand. Tilly hopped on.

'Let's go!' she said.

The crescent moon was white in the darkening evening sky. A chill breeze made Mike shiver.

'Ah!' said Tilly. 'This feels better.'

By the light of a torch, Mike took her along a garden path to a wooden shed, where the lawnmower, roller and tools were kept.

'You'll be safe here,' he told her. 'You can make a nest in this basket. Here are a couple of old blankets and a cushion.'

Mike went back to the house and fetched half a loaf of brown bread and a bowl of water.

'We let Oliver out at night,' he said, 'but I'll make sure the shed door is properly closed.'

'I'd appreciate that tonight,' Tilly said. 'By tomorrow there'll be no problem.'

Mike wondered what she meant. Was it his imagination, or had she already grown since her arrival? When she got out of the packet she was the size of a sparrow. Now she seemed as big as a pigeon.

Back in the house, Mike let Oliver into the kitchen and gave him some sardine-flavoured Yummies and milk.

Mike's parents came home late. He had stayed awake to talk to his mother. When she came to his room to say goodnight, he said:

14

'I bet you can't guess what I got today. A pterodactyl!'

'A what?'

'A pterodactyl. Her name is Tilly. She's a sort of bird, with a lizard's body and bat-wings. She says she's millions of years old, but she looks young. She loves jam.'

His mother laughed.

'You've been dreaming,' she said, and went downstairs.

'What was the big joke?' his father asked. She told him, and they both laughed.

'I suppose it's something he saw on TV,' he said.

Mike heard the laughter. If that was their attitude, he thought, he would not mention Tilly again.

The next morning, Mike took a large box of Crunch-Nut breakfast food from the kitchen cupboard and hurried to the garden shed.

The basket was empty.

'Don't be alarmed,' said a voice like Tilly's but deeper than before. 'Here I am.'

Mike turned. There, behind the lawnmower, stood Tilly. During the night, she had grown much bigger. Now she was almost as tall as a pony.

He was so astonished at first that he was

unable to speak.

'It's all right,' she said soothingly.
'This is my full size.' And she spread her

17

wings and flapped them. From tip to tip, they were as wide as a piano.

'Wow!' Mike exclaimed. 'You must be able to fly really high with those.'

'And fast.'

'I've brought you some Crunch-Nut.

But you'll need more than that, won't you?'

'Yes, I'm quite peckish. I was wondering what cats taste like?'

'Tilly, you wouldn't! We've had Oliver since he was a kitten.'

'Don't worry. I was only joking. I'd never hurt any friend of yours.'

'I'll go to the shops and buy you some food. I've got a bit of money saved up.'

Mike ran all the way. He bought a big pork pie, a selection of sliced meats, a long loaf of French bread, a bag of jam-filled doughnuts, a bunch of bananas, a kilo of assorted nuts, a bar of chocolate and a litre bottle of lemonade.

Chapter 2

MIKE INTENDED TO keep Tilly secret on Monday. But when you go to school with a secret as fantastic as that, it is very difficult not to share it. How could you possibly stop yourself from telling your friends if you are keeping a pterodactyl, millions of years old, that knows a lot and speaks excellent English?

During the first lesson of the day, Mike raised his hand to ask a question.

'Yes, Mike?' said the teacher, Mr Calliper.

'When was the last time anyone in England saw a pterodactyl?' Mike asked.

'Nobody in England has ever seen a pterodactyl,' Mr Calliper said, 'for the simple reason that pterodactyls lived long before there were any people.'

'Well, I've seen one.'

All the other children burst out laughing.

'Very funny, Mike,' Mr Calliper said, slightly irritably. 'However, the subject we are discussing is computers. So –'

'Really, Mr Calliper, it's true. She's staying in our garden. She's about four feet tall, and her wings are about eight feet wide.'

Again the children laughed.

'That's enough!' the teacher said, warningly holding up a hand. 'If you want to discuss prehistoric creatures, Mike, wait for Natural History.'

'But –'

'But nothing, Mike. Back to computers. . .'

In the playground during the mid-morning break, even Mike's friends made fun of him and his claim.

'It's hard to believe that you've got a terro-what-do-you-call-it at home,' said Diana, who liked Mike and wanted to believe him.

'Pterodactyl,' he insisted. 'Her name is Tilly. She's millions of years old. An

Eskimo fisherman caught her accidentally.'

'How do you know?'

'She told me.'

'A terro-thingummy *told* you?' jeered Bruce. 'Don't be stupid.'

'Tilly speaks as well as you and me.' Mike said.

Just then, he noticed the dreaded Rodney, the school bully, coming their way.

'Liar! Liar!' he shouted as he got near. 'Mike Verity is a liar!'
Mike blushed red. He felt like punching Rodney for making everyone stare at him. But the bell rang to signal the end of break and time for the next lesson. It was just as well.

By the end of school, Mike had had enough teasing and insults for one day, so he left for home immediately.

Chapter 3

As Mike walked through the garden gate, he heard a spitting, howling noise from the direction of the shed. Oliver had found Tilly! After one look at the size of her, he had turned and run. Tilly watched him streaking across the lawn in a panic and falling into the goldfish pond with a loud splash.

Mike rushed forward to help, but he was not nearly as quick as Tilly. With one beat of her wings, she swooped to the side of the pond and lifted Oliver out of the water, as a cat lifts a kitten, by the scruff of the neck. Oliver was dazed and limp and dripping as Tilly swung him clear of the pond and deposited him on the grass. Mike carried him into the house and dried him with a towel. Oliver seemed pleased to return to the quiet comfort of Gran's room.

'*There* you are!' Mike's grandmother said with a sigh. 'Been out hunting, have you, Oliver?' Oliver purred and jumped on to her lap. He settled down and Gran stroked him.

Back in the shed, Mike gave Tilly a big meal, including a whole pizza, and praised her for her quick thinking and gallant action. Then he told her everything about

his bad day at school, especially how horrible Rodney had been.

'That's tough,' Tilly commented at last. 'I'd like to teach that Rodney a lesson.'

'Yes,' Mike said. 'But how?'

'That's easy,' said Tilly.

By the time she had explained her plan, Mike felt so excited he could hardly wait for the next day.

Chapter 4

THE FOLLOWING MORNING, Mike was not at school. His classmates wondered why. There was a buzz of talk about him.

'Perhaps he's ill,' Diana suggested.

'Or can't face us,' Bruce said. 'We weren't very nice to him.'

'Mike's feeling like a fool,' Rodney said, 'because that's what he is.'

At 11 o'clock, the bell rang for break, and the children ran out to the playground.

Mike isn't only a liar and a fool,' Rodney said with a crooked smile. 'He's a coward.'

'He is *not* a coward!' Diana shouted back.

Then there was a loud flapping, as if a whole flock of geese were approaching.

Everyone looked up.

High above the school's red-tiled roof was Tilly, with Mike sitting astride her, like a jockey mounted well forward on a racehorse. He was gripping Tilly firmly with his knees, with his arms around her neck.

Tilly flapped her great wings and swooped over the playground.

Then down she plunged, like an eagle falling on its prey. She dived at Rodney, fiercely squawking at him, pecking at his ears, again and again. Yelping with fear, blubbing like a baby, Rodney ran away. Tilly followed, flapping her wings close to his head. At the edge of the playground she turned and zoomed upward again, while Rodney scuttled into the school.

He ran to his classroom, where Mr Calliper was sitting at his desk, writing notes.

31

'Mike's bird tried to kill me!' Rodney cried. 'It's a monster! Call the police!'

'Slow down, Rodney,' Mr Calliper said. 'Now what's all this about?'

'It's the pterodactyl!'

'Nonsense, boy!' Mr Calliper said. 'Now sit here quietly and read while I go and investigate.'

He got to the playground as Tilly was
performing some sensational low-level
stunts – diving and zooming, twisting and
rolling, looping the loop, flying upside
down, at top speed. The children were
cheering and waving and Mike was
triumphantly waving back.

Mr Calliper was amazed. He ran inside

again, and down the hall to the office, and told the headmistress what he had seen. By the time he had persuaded her to look for herself, the playground was deserted.

'Calm down, Mr Calliper,' the headmistress said. 'Pull yourself together. You've been imagining things. Perhaps you need a rest. Anyway, the bell has gone. The children are back in their classrooms. You'd better get back to yours.'

When Mr Calliper returned to his room, he found Tilly at his place by the blackboard. She was giving the class a lesson about dinosaurs.

'Judging by your questions,' she was saying, 'I must say you've been taught a lot of rubbish. The dinosaurs did not rule the world, and they certainly were not at all intelligent. They were giants, but they were clumsy and very, very silly. They

35

spent the whole time fighting each other, killing each other, until there weren't any of them left.'

Standing in the doorway, Mr Calliper could hardly believe what he saw and heard. There was a terrible noise in the classroom. The children were all shouting excitedly. The other teachers came running to see what had happened.

'Please, children!' said the headmistress, and they all quietened down.

'Where's the pterodactyl?' Mr Calliper asked.

The children all answered at once.

'Quiet!' Mr Calliper shouted. 'Where is Mike Verity?'

'He flew home,' said Diana.

Mr Calliper turned to the headmistress. 'I have a headache and I think I'm going crazy,' he said.

'No you're not,' she said. 'You're just
tired.' And turning to the class she added:
'Settle down now children. We're going
to have a special lesson now – making
dinosaurs.' And she went to the cupboard
and took out pencils and paints, cardboard
and plasticine.

Mr Calliper handed them round and
took The Big Book of Dinosaurs off the
shelf. He propped it up for everyone to
see, and the fun began.

Chapter 5

'THAT WAS FABULOUS!' Mike said to
Tilly after they had landed in the garden.
'Thanks a lot.'

'It was a pleasure,' she said. 'I like your friends. But you know I'm not used to crowds. I miss the wide open spaces of the Far North. Of course, this place might be all right for a different pterodactyl.'

When his mother returned from the hairdresser's and his father returned from work, Mike told them about his day. Mr and Mrs Verity exchanged smiles and shrugged their shoulders, as if they thought he was making everything up.

'You still don't believe me, do you?' Mike said. 'It's easy to prove I've told you the truth. Come on. I'll show you.'

The door of the shed was wide open. Tilly was not inside.

Mike was dismayed.

'She was here only a few minutes ago,' he said.

His parents smiled doubtfully.

Mike felt awful. He looked around the

deserted shed.

And then he saw it!

On the cushion in the middle of the basket, there was a most extraordinary egg. It was a lot bigger than a hen's egg, and it was coloured orange and pink!

Handling it with care, Mike held it up

and smiled. His mother and father looked mystified.

'You'll believe me,' he said, 'when this hatches.'